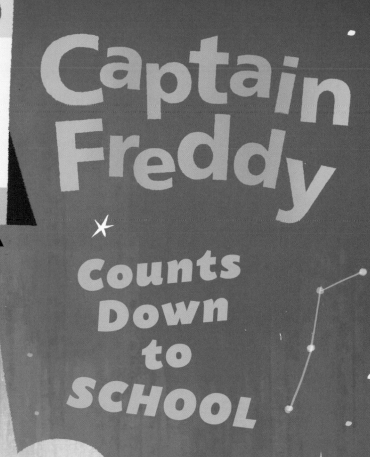

Captain Freddy

Counts Down to SCHOOL

BY
ELIZABETH SHREEVE

SPACE FACTS

ILLUSTRATED BY
JOEY CHOU

Peachtree

two lions

It's Freddy's very first day of school.
"Are you ready?" calls Mom.

"Almost," says Freddy.
He closes the door.

He crawls under
the covers.

SPACE
FACTS

School is big.
It's far, far away.
And it's full of strangers.
So before he leaves home . . .

. . . Captain Freddy has important work to do at his space station.

Rocket ship loaded?
CHECK!

Fuel tanks full?
CHECK!

SPACE

Engines humming?
CHECK!

All systems are go for . . .

"School time!" calls Mom.
"Put on your new shoes!"

"Roger," says Freddy.
He pulls on
his moon boots.

He steps onto
the launch pad.

He starts to count.

"Ten . . .

nine . . .

eight . . ."

"And a clean shirt!" calls Mom.

"Got it," says Freddy.
He buttons his uniform.
He straps on his laser.

"Seven . . .

six . . .

five . . .

four . . ."

SPACE FACTS

"Don't forget your backpack!" calls Mom.

"**All set,**" says Freddy. He tightens his jet pack.

"*Three . . .*

two . . .

ONE . . ."

LIFTOFF!

Freddy's rocket ship zooms
past the moon . . .
straight for the stars . . .
far, far away.

"**Full power!**" yells Freddy.
The ship starts to spin.
It veers off course.

Faster, faster.
It's out of control—**it's about to explode!**

Eject, EJECT!

WHOOSH!

In the nick of time,
Captain Freddy fires his jet pack.
The ship spirals away.
A narrow escape!

Now he tumbles
through space,
all alone.

KER-PLOOM!

Captain Freddy lands on
a faraway planet,
millions and millions
of miles from home.

His jet pack is squished.
His ship is long gone.
And just when things couldn't get
any worse, over the horizon comes . . .

. . . an alien!

"*Goo-lub-lub!*" it bellows,
and grabs for Freddy's laser.

They wrestle! They run!
The alien gets away!

But luckily . . .

. . . Captain Freddy remembers
that he can speak alien, too.
"Ooo-goo-baa!" he shouts.
"Ka-zeeba-galook!"

The alien grins.
"Badada, goo-bee?"

"Aha!" says Freddy,
and hands over his laser.

Mom opens the door.
"Freddy, what's going on?
I've been calling and calling.
Sometimes I think you're in
outer space."

"I was," says Freddy.
"And I met this alien.
We were chasing each other,
but now we're friends."

"Great," says Mom.
"But tell me, Freddy.
Are you finally ready for—"

"Of course," says Freddy.
"School's a big place, Mom.
But I've been to space, and it is gigantic.
So come on, let's hurry.
It's time to blast off to school!"

CAPTAIN FREDDY'S SPACE FACTS

Our planet, Earth, is part of a solar system. The solar system has eight planets that orbit around the sun.

The **BIGGEST** object in our solar system is the sun. The sun is a hot, glowing star. Its warmth and light keep all the plants and animals on Earth alive.

SUN

MERCURY

The **SMALLEST** planet in our solar system is Mercury. Like Earth, it is one of the four inner "rocky planets."

VENUS

The **SPARKLIEST** planet in our solar system is Saturn. It is famous for its bright, swirling rings. The rings consist of icy rocks and dust.

The **HOTTEST** planet in our solar system is Venus. It is about the same size as Earth, but it's much, much hotter.

SATURN

JUPITER

The **BIGGEST** planet in our solar system is Jupiter. It is so huge that all the other planets in the solar system could fit inside it.

The **CLOSEST** object to Earth is the moon. The moon orbits around Earth. Astronauts have traveled to the moon in about four days—and have even walked on it!

MOON

EARTH

The **WETTEST** planet in our solar system is Earth. It's the only planet with large oceans and air that we can breathe.

The **LITTLE KIDS** of the solar system are the dwarf planets. These small planets are named Ceres, Pluto, Haumea, Makemake, and Eris.

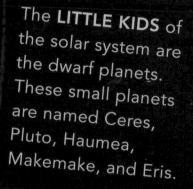

CERES

ERIS

HAUMEA

The **REDDEST** planet in our solar system is Mars. It looks red because its soil contains a lot of iron oxide (rust).

MARS

MAKEMAKE

The **FARTHEST** planets are Uranus and Neptune. Neptune is the most distant planet from the sun. Uranus is tipped on its side. Scientists believe that a huge space object may have crashed into it long ago.

PLUTO

URANUS ## NEPTUNE

For Sam, the original space captain! —E.S.

For Mom, and all our wonderful adventurous walks to school! —J.C.

Bibliography and Further Reading

WEBSITES:

http://www.enchantedlearning.com/subjects/astronomy/planets/jupiter/moons.shtml

http://www.funology.com/facts-about-outer-space/

http://listverse.com/2007/11/13/top-10-cool-facts-about-space/

http://oceanservice.noaa.gov/facts/et-oceans.html

http://planetfacts.org/temperature-of-the-sun/

http://www.nasa.gov/audience/forkids/kidsclub/text/games/levelfive/KC_Solar_System.html#.VZqKnkZk6qg

http://www.nasa.gov/returntoflight/system/system_ET.html

http://www.nasa.gov/centers/jpl/education/spaceprobe-20100225.html

http://www.science-facts.com/quick-facts/amazing-outer-space-facts/

http://www.sciencekids.co.nz/sciencefacts/space/solarsystem.html

http://www.universetoday.com/30534/what-is-a-galaxy/

BOOKS:

Branley, Franklyn M. *The Planets in Our Solar System.* New York: HarperCollins, 1998

Cole, Joanna. *The Magic School Bus: Lost in the Solar System.* New York: Scholastic Press, 1990

Graham, Ian. *My Book of Space.* New York: Kingfisher, 2001

Hughes, Catherine D. *Little Kids First Big Book of Space.* Washington, DC: National Geographic Children's Books, 2012

Stott, Carole. *Space Exploration.* New York: DK Eyewitness Books, 2014

Text copyright © 2016 by Elizabeth Shreeve

Illustrations copyright © 2016 by Joey Chou

Published by Two Lions, New York

www.apub.com

Amazon, the Amazon logo, and Two Lions are trademarks of Amazon.com, Inc., or its affiliates.

ISBN-13: 9781503950955 (hardcover)

ISBN-10: 1503950956 (hardcover)

ISBN-13: 9781503950221 (paperback)

ISBN-10: 1503950220 (paperback)

The illustrations are rendered in digital media.

Printed in China (R)

First edition

10 9 8 7 6 5 4 3 2 1